TABLE OF CONTENTS

BY JAKE MADDOX

illustrated by Sean Tiffany

text by Bob Temple

Librarian Reviewer
Chris Kreie
Media Specialist, Eden Prairie Schools, MN
MS in Information Media, St. Cloud State University, MN

Reading Consultant
Mary Evenson
Middle School Teacher, Edina Public Schools, MN
MA in Education, University of Minnesota

STONE ARCH BOOKS
www.stonearchbooks.com

Impact Books are published by Stone Arch Books
151 Good Counsel Drive, P.O. Box 669
Mankato, Minnesota 56002
www.stonearchbooks.com

Library of Congress Cataloging-in-Publication Data
Maddox, Jake.
    Takedown / by Jake Maddox; illustrated by Sean Tiffany.
    p. cm. — (Impact Books. A Jake Maddox Sports Story)
    ISBN 978-1-4342-0774-6 (library binding)
    ISBN 978-1-4342-0870-5 (pbk.)
    [1. Wrestling—Fiction. 2. Self-control—Fiction.] I. Tiffany, Sean,
ill. II. Title.
PZ7.M25643Tak 2009
[Fic]—dc2   2008004298

Summary: Jeff wants to be a good wrestler, but will his bad temper get
in the way?

Art Director: Heather Kindseth
Graphic Designer: Kay Fraser

1 2 3 4 5 6 13 12 11 10 09 08

Printed in the United States of America

LOSING IT

The basement door swung wide open. "Jeff! Jeff, Jeff, Jeff!" a voice screamed. It was Caleb, Jeff Carter's five-year-old brother. He ran into the room and started bouncing up and down on the couch.

Caleb wasn't the worst little brother in the world, but Jeff was often annoyed by him. The kid was always running around and being loud — two things that drove Jeff crazy.

"Leave me alone," Jeff said. "Come on, Caleb. Go away!"

Caleb ignored him. He jumped off the couch. Then he walked over and looked at the TV.

"What are you playing?" he asked. "Are you winning?"

Jeff sighed. He tried to keep his focus on the snowboarder on the TV screen.

"Yes, I'm winning," he said. He paused the game and turned to look at Caleb. "I'm just about to set a new record, but I'm coming to the hardest part right now," he added.

Caleb climbed onto the couch next to Jeff. He kept bouncing up and down, making weird sounds, and getting on Jeff's nerves.

"What's the record?" Caleb asked. "Are you going to break it for sure, Jeff? Do you really think you can do it? Huh, Jeff? Can you for sure?"

"Yes, I can do it," Jeff said. "I'm way ahead. I just need to get through the last part of the run, and I'll have the best time and the most points I've ever gotten in this game."

"Can I watch?" Caleb said. Jeff ignored him. "Can I watch?" Caleb said, louder.

Jeff sighed. "Yes, you can watch," he said, trying to be nice. "But you have to sit still."

"Okay, I will," Caleb promised.

Jeff unpaused the game. His character continued down the run, making great turns and jumps along the way.

Jeff's thumbs bounced over the game controller. On the TV screen in front of him, a snowboarder swerved down a challenging course.

The snowboarder was making record time. He flew through the air over rocks that stuck out of the snow.

Jeff was on the edge of his seat. His muscular body reacted to everything on the screen. When the snowboarder needed to turn left, Jeff leaned to the left. When the snowboarder needed to jump, Jeff lifted his body up ever so slightly.

At one point, the snowboarder appeared to be coming down from a jump too early. Jeff leaned and lifted the controller a little, as if that would help keep his character up in the air.

It seemed to work. The snowboarder barely made it.

"Yes!" Jeff blurted out. "That was awesome!"

Finally, he headed into the most difficult part. It was full of hairpin turns, tunnels, jumps, and other obstacles.

Jeff passed the first obstacles easily. He knew he was on his way to setting the record. He could practically taste victory.

"Look out!" Caleb yelled as Jeff headed into a tunnel.

Coming out the other side, Jeff went off a jump that sent his character flying. He would have to be careful to control the landing, or he'd lose for sure.

"Oh no!" Caleb screamed.

Then Caleb jumped out of his seat and ran to the television set. He stood directly in front of the screen.

"Hey!" Jeff yelled. "Get out of my way!"

But it was too late. Caleb was blocking the screen, so Jeff couldn't see enough of the course to keep his guy out of trouble.

Jeff's character crashed into a snow bank. Jeff gasped. "Oh, no," he whispered. He quickly tried to fix the mess. But it was no use. The record was gone.

Jeff felt the heat rise into his face. He stood up. "Caleb!" he yelled. "You little brat! You wrecked my game!"

"I did not!" Caleb yelled back.

Jeff slammed his controller on the ground. In a flash, he was on top of Caleb, holding him in a headlock.

"You always ruin everything," Jeff told Caleb. "I was about to set the record!"

"I didn't ruin anything!" Caleb yelled.

"You'll be sorry," Jeff said.

The basement door opened. It was their mother. "Jeffrey! Let go of him right now!" she screamed.

CHAPTER 2

SOMEONE YOUR OWN SIZE

Jeff was sent directly to his room. He sat there for more than an hour, his anger slowly draining away.

He didn't get why his mother was so upset. He hadn't really hurt Caleb. He just wanted to show his brother how mad he was.

After a while, Jeff wasn't angry anymore. Then his mother knocked on the bedroom door. She walked in.

"Jeffrey," she said, "you need to apologize to Caleb."

Jeff looked at Caleb, who was peeking through the doorway. "I'm sorry for putting you in a headlock when you wrecked my chances for the record," Jeff said.

Caleb smiled at him. Jeff rolled his eyes.

"I know that all brothers argue sometimes," Jeff's mother said. "But your temper has really gotten out of control. You're much bigger than Caleb, and you could really hurt him, even if you don't mean to."

"Yeah," Caleb chimed in. His grin was really wide.

"You've got to control yourself," his mother went on. "You shouldn't pick on your little brother."

"Pick on someone your own size," Caleb said.

"I am not picking on him," said Jeff. "He wrecked my game!"

"I think you two should do something fun together this afternoon," Mom said. "Why don't you go to the park? Caleb would love that."

"Yeah!" Caleb shouted. "Let's go to the park and play Shark Attack!"

That sounded like the opposite of fun to Jeff. "Aw, come on, Mom!" he said. "I'm not his babysitter."

But his mother insisted. So, fifteen minutes later, the brothers were at the park, and Jeff was pushing Caleb on the swings. He played tag with him. They went down the slide.

Jeff even agreed to play the game Caleb had made up. It was called "Shark Attack." To play it, they pretended that the sand was an ocean, full of sharks that they had to hide from.

Finally, after an hour, Jeff said, "Well, I think it's time to go home, don't you, Caleb?"

Caleb shook his head and frowned. "No," Caleb whined. "I want to play Shark Attack again."

"We've already done that a million times," Jeff said.

"No!" Caleb yelled. He ran to the slide.

Jeff walked over to the swings and sat down in one. He figured that if he didn't play with Caleb, his brother would get bored and agree to leave.

At the other side of the park, a group of guys was standing around. A couple of them looked familiar.

Jeff knew that one of the guys was a kid named Logan, who went to his school. He wasn't sure who the others were.

Suddenly, Jeff felt something hit his head. Then something else. He turned and looked around. Caleb was throwing pebbles at him.

Jeff could hear his brother giggling. He tried to ignore Caleb, but that was getting harder to do.

Finally, Caleb sneaked up behind Jeff. Then the little boy dumped a whole bucket of sand over his brother's head.

"That's it!" Jeff screamed. "I've had enough of you!"

In an instant, Jeff was running after him. Caleb screamed happily as he ran away. But this was no game to Jeff. He was mad. "I'll get you!" he yelled.

Suddenly, Jeff was flat on his stomach in the sand. He'd been knocked over by a tackle. Some other kid had jumped on top of him, pinning one of his arms behind his back.

Jeff was powerless.

"Hey," the tackler said into Jeff's ear. "Why don't you stop being such a bully and pick on someone your own size?"

CHAPTER 3

TEMPER

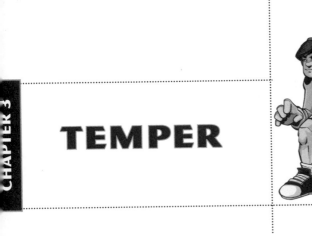

Angrily, Jeff struggled to get free. But every time he tried to move, the tackler's grip got tighter.

Jeff tried everything he could think of to escape. Finally, he realized there was no point, and he relaxed a little.

Then the tackler flipped him over with a quick, powerful move. He pinned Jeff's shoulders to the sand.

Jeff stared up at his attacker.

The tackler was Logan Jackson, the guy Jeff had recognized from school. He was a year older than Jeff, but Jeff had seen him in the hallways sometimes.

"Get off me!" Jeff demanded.

"Are you going to go after that kid?" Logan asked calmly.

"He's my little brother," Jeff explained. "Besides, it's none of your business."

Jeff heard Caleb giggling nearby.

"You have quite a temper," Logan said.

Jeff struggled to get up, but it was pretty obvious that he couldn't. He relaxed a little, and Logan's hold relaxed too. Soon, Jeff felt his anger slipping away, as it had when he was sitting alone in his bedroom. He just lay there, wishing Logan would let go of him.

"Are you going to let me up or not?"
Jeff asked.

Logan got up. Jeff sat up slowly, rubbing
his shoulders.

"Here," Logan said, reaching out
a hand.

Jeff glared at him. "No thanks, I'm fine,"
he said. Then he scrambled to his feet and
brushed the sand out of his hair and off
his shoulders.

Jeff could tell that Logan was staring at
him. He looked up and stared directly back
at Logan. Neither of them said a word.

Then Caleb came up and took Jeff by
the hand. "Come on, Jeff. Let's go home!"
he said.

"Okay," Jeff said.

The two brothers turned and walked away.

As they left the park, Jeff looked back over his shoulder. He saw Logan walking away, too, holding the hand of his own little brother.

The next morning, Jeff walked through the school door. As he did, he slammed into another student.

"Watch it!" shouted Jeff. Then he saw that the person he'd bumped into was Logan Jackson.

"Sorry," Jeff said quickly. "I didn't see you there."

"No problem," Logan said. "I was looking for you anyway."

Jeff felt the hair stand up on the back of his neck. He clenched his fists. If he had to fight, he was ready.

"Easy," Logan said. "I'm not coming after you. I just want to talk."

Jeff didn't know what to say. "Why?" he asked.

"I thought I should apologize about the park yesterday," Logan said. "I thought you were going to really hurt your brother. I'd never seen anyone look as angry as you did. So I just kind of reacted."

"Whatever," Jeff said. He slowly unclenched his fists.

"Listen," Logan said. "You fought pretty hard. You're strong."

"Yeah, so what?" Jeff said. "What's your point?"

"My point is, I think you should try out for the wrestling team," Logan said. "Practice starts next week. We could use someone with your strength."

Jeff wasn't sure what to say. He'd never thought about trying out for a sport before. "Um, maybe," he said.

"Seriously, you should," Logan said. "Some of us guys are going to meet for workouts before school this week. I'm one of the captains of the Pirates. If you want to try it out, meet us in the gym tomorrow morning at 6:30. I think you could be good at it."

"Okay," Jeff said. "I'll give it a try."

CHAPTER 5

THINGS TO LEARN

Aside from getting up so early that first morning, Jeff didn't have any trouble with the wrestling workouts. In fact, he thought they were a relaxing way to start his day.

The workouts always started with some light exercises. Then all of the guys lifted weights for a while before heading off to class.

Jeff liked the workouts. He also liked most of the guys on the team.

Logan and a few of the other guys were really serious about wrestling. Sometimes, Jeff thought they seemed too serious. But Jeff figured they were just trying to be the leaders of the team, since they were the captains. They were pretty cool, and they made the workouts fun.

The following Monday was the first day of real practice. After school, all the guys headed for the locker room, where they changed into their workout clothes and weighed in. Jeff weighed in at 105 pounds.

After everyone had weighed in, Coach Flood led the boys outside. They all went on a two-mile run around the football field.

At the end of the run, Jeff was panting and really tired. But the day wasn't close to being over yet.

Next, they went to the wrestling room. There, they did so many push-ups and sit-ups that Jeff lost count.

After a short water break, Coach Flood split the guys into pairs according to their weight. Jeff was paired up with a guy named Luis, who had been on the team for the last three years.

"You're new to the team, right?" Luis asked.

Jeff nodded. "Yeah," he said. "Never wrestled before in my life. I'm a good fighter, though."

"Cool," Luis said. "I'll show you the opening stance when we get out on the mat," he offered.

Jeff smiled. "Thanks," he said. "I guess I have some stuff to learn."

On the mat, Luis quickly showed Jeff how to stand. Both of them crouched down, facing each other, with their knees bent and their hands outstretched.

Then the whistle blew. Luis and Jeff moved around their circle, carefully eyeing each other. Luis made a couple of fast, fake moves toward Jeff. No big deal.

Suddenly, without warning, Luis pounced. He sprang toward Jeff's legs, and was so quick and powerful that Jeff didn't have time to react. Luis locked up both of Jeff's legs and drove him down to the mat, hard. Jeff was pinned. He hadn't even seen it coming.

After he walked off the mat, Jeff looked up at the clock. It was only 4:15. Practice was only halfway over! Jeff didn't think he'd make it until 5 p.m.

CHAPTER 6

STRENGTH AND SPEED

By the end of practice, Jeff was exhausted. His muscles had never been worked so hard.

Before Jeff could change and get out of the locker room, Logan sat down next to him on the locker room bench.

"Learn anything today?" Logan asked.

Jeff nodded. "I learned that I stink at wrestling," he said.

"You do stink," Logan said, waving his hand in front of his face. "Phew!"

Both of them laughed. "Yeah, I need a shower," Jeff said.

He paused, looking down at his feet. Then Jeff admitted, "I guess I just don't really know what I'm doing out there. Every time I think I do, I find out I don't."

"Don't worry," Logan replied. "We'll take care of that."

Over the next few weeks, Logan worked closely with Jeff every day during wrestling practice.

He helped Jeff with his takedown moves, his holds, and how to use his body to push against his opponent. They also worked on escape moves for when Jeff was about to be pinned.

Jeff felt more confident, but he hadn't wrestled against a real opponent yet. He had no idea what would happen when he stepped onto the mat for a real match. He hated to admit it, but he was pretty nervous.

One night, Coach Flood gathered all the players onto the mat.

"As you all know, we face the Evanston Eagles on Thursday," the coach said. "After practice tonight, I'll post the list for the first meet. I have each of you in the best weight class for you. I think we're all ready to start the season, and the Pirates have a great chance to win in this meet."

For the rest of practice, Jeff was nervous. He wasn't sure what to expect. Logan was still working with him, and he felt like he was getting better.

But Logan had been wrestling for years. He also weighed twenty pounds more than Jeff did. That allowed him to control Jeff when they really tried to compete.

The problem with practicing with Logan was that it was never really a fair fight. Jeff didn't know whether he'd improved or not.

The worst part was that he didn't know what might happen when he wrestled against a more experienced wrestler in his own weight class.

After school, he caught up with Logan as they both walked home.

"You ready for your first meet?" asked Logan.

Jeff shrugged. "Kind of, I guess," he said. Then he asked, "Do you know the guy I'm wrestling against?"

"Yeah, I do," Logan said. "The 105-pound guy from Evanston is this kid named Brandon."

"So what should I be looking out for?" Jeff asked. "How can I get ready?"

Logan frowned, thinking. "I've never wrestled him," he said finally. "But I've seen him in action, and he's really fast. That'll be the main thing to look out for. Speed. Because he can sneak up on you, and he'll do it."

"Okay, speed," Jeff said, nodding. "I can handle that. What else should I know about Brandon?"

"The other thing is that he's strong," Logan said. "But you're strong too, so that shouldn't be a problem. Just look out for his speed."

Logan paused, and then added, "I always watch the other guy's eyes. If I see him glance down, I figure he's going for my knees. And most of the time, I'm right."

"Thanks for the tip," said Jeff.

"No problem," Logan said. "I think you've got a good chance to win your first match!"

FIRST MEET

The next day, Jeff was nervous. It was the day of the first meet between the Pirates and the Eagles. Jeff tried to ignore how packed the gym was when he walked in that afternoon.

He spotted his mom and Caleb sitting in the bleachers. His mom waved at him, but Jeff was too nervous to wave back. He tried to smile, but he was even too nervous to to do that.

The wrestlers would compete in periods that lasted two minutes. The first wrestler to pin the other wrestler or win two periods would win the match.

The first few matches flew by. Jeff tried to stay calm. When it was time for his match, he took a deep breath, unzipped his sweatshirt, and tried to focus.

He tried to ignore the other wrestlers and everyone else in the gym. He just thought about what he had learned.

Jeff stepped onto the mat and moved into position. Then Brandon walked out to the mat. He was a little taller than Jeff, and it seemed like he had more muscles.

Jeff got nervous again. He shook hands with Brandon. Then they both got into position.

The whistle blew. Jeff and Brandon locked arms together. They began to move around the circle.

Brandon didn't waste any time. He moved quickly for Jeff's right leg.

Jeff was ready for him. He had seen Brandon's eyes glance quickly downward.

Jeff pulled his right leg back and pushed down on Brandon with his upper body, forcing him face-first into the mat.

Now Jeff was on top of Brandon. Jeff controlled one of Brandon's arms and locked up one of his legs. Brandon was strong, though. He quickly got control back.

The two guys wrestled for the rest of the first period. Neither of them were able to do much. At the end of the period, neither seemed ahead.

When the whistle blew, Jeff felt disappointed. He didn't think he'd done very well. Then he heard Logan's voice.

"Way to go, Jeff!" Logan called. "You won the round!"

Jeff was thrilled. The takedown on Brandon had earned Jeff two points. Even though he hadn't been able to pin Brandon, Jeff had still won the period.

Now he just needed to win the next one. Then he'd win the match.

At the start of the second period, Brandon immediately took Jeff down. Jeff was able to pull himself up, but he felt a burst of anger streak through his body.

His face felt hot, and he struggled angrily to get out of Brandon's grasp. But Brandon held him down.

Jeff started to lose focus. Instead of remembering any escape moves, he just felt mad that he wasn't winning.

Suddenly, he was lying on his back.

"Pin!" the referee yelled.

Jeff jumped up. He ran into the locker room. He started slamming his locker door over and over.

Then Logan came in. He rushed over and grabbed Jeff's arm. He pushed Jeff away from the locker.

"Pull yourself together! What's your problem?" Logan yelled.

"I can't believe I let that guy beat me," Jeff muttered.

Logan sighed. "You were doing great," he said. "Right up until you got mad."

Jeff crossed his arms and leaned back against the lockers. "So what are you saying?" he said angrily. "Should I be happy when I lose?"

"Of course not. I'm just saying that Brandon didn't pin you until you got mad," Logan pointed out. "You were doing fine. Just use that anger in a different way. Instead of getting all upset at the other guy, use all that extra energy to escape."

Then Logan smiled. "Haven't you figured it out yet? You can't win when you're mad."

CHAPTER 8

KEEPING CONTROL

As he walked home after the match that evening, Jeff thought about what Logan had said.

Logan had been completely right. The second Jeff had gotten angry, he had started to lose control.

Was it that simple? Could Jeff win, if he controlled his anger? Could he win if he pushed his anger in a different direction? Would it work?

When he got home, Jeff went down to the basement TV room. A little time with his video games was exactly what he needed to calm down after the stressful wrestling meet.

He sat down onto the couch and turned on the TV. But as his videogame booted up, Caleb ran into the room. He slammed the basement door behind him.

"What are you doing, Jeff?" Caleb asked, smiling. He hopped up onto the couch next to Jeff and peered at the TV.

Jeff sighed. He couldn't even get five minutes of peace. But he tried to keep his cool.

"I'm going to try for the record on the snowboarding game again," he told Caleb. "Are you going to sit here and be quiet and watch, or are you going to get in my way?"

"Just watch," Caleb said, a big grin on his face.

"You can stay if you promise not to get off the couch," said Jeff.

Caleb nodded happily. "Okay," he said.

On the screen, the game began. Right away, the snowboarder really got going. Jeff was on fire. His fingers flew over the controller, and his whole body was tense as he led the snowboarder around obstacles and down steep jumps.

After about twenty minutes, Jeff was the closest he'd ever been to his record. When he came to an easier part of the course, he glanced over to see why Caleb was being so quiet.

Just then, Caleb jumped up and screamed.

Jeff was so surprised that he dropped the controller on the ground.

Caleb burst into laughter. "I scared you, Jeffy!" he yelled. "I scared you bad!"

On the television screen, Jeff's snowboarder flew off a jump and landed on his back in the snow.

GAME OVER flashed on the screen.

Jeff felt his face turning red. "I'm going to get you this time," he growled at Caleb. "I really am." He slowly started to get up from the couch, keeping his eyes on Caleb.

Then he saw a look of fear pass over his little brother's face.

Jeff moved closer to Caleb. When he was standing right in front of Caleb, he leaned down, very slowly, until he was at Caleb's level.

Then he attacked. Moving quickly, he scooped the little boy up and started tickling his armpits.

"That's what you get!" Jeff teased his brother, who was screaming with laughter. "You get in my way, and the tickle monster comes to get you!"

Caleb was still screeching happily when the basement door swung open, banging into the wall.

"Jeff!" his mom screamed. "He's only five! Stop hurting him!"

Caleb stopped laughing. He and Jeff both looked at their mom. Then Caleb said, "Mom, he's not hurting me! Jeff is the tickle monster!"

Jeff smiled. "I'm not hurting him, Mom," he said. "We're having fun."

Jeff's mother looked shocked. "Oh," was all she said.

Caleb said. "Jeff's really strong!"

"I know he is," Mom replied. "And when he doesn't get mad, he can do anything!"

Jeff smiled again. Then he remembered what Logan had said. Maybe controlling his anger would help him after all.

FIGURING IT OUT

The next weekend, the Pirates were in a huge tournament. Even though Jeff hadn't won a match yet, he was pretty excited. Eight schools were in the tournament, and Coach Flood thought their team had a real shot to take the championship.

The early matches went well. Jeff's team wasn't in first place, but they were doing well. All of the wrestlers were feeling good about their chances.

Just before the first 105-pound match, Coach Flood pulled Jeff aside. "Okay, Jeff," the coach said. "You're wrestling Marcus. He's from Springhill. The Springhill Stallions are tough in every class. So here's what I want from you."

Jeff lowered his head and listened carefully.

Coach Flood said, "The Pirates are going to need every point we can get against the Stallions. So in this match, it doesn't matter if you win. Marcus is a very experienced wrestler, and while I think you have a lot of potential, he might have more power than you. You just have to make sure that he doesn't pin you. If he pins you, they get six points. But if you fight him off — even if you lose the match — the score will be much closer."

Jeff understood, but he didn't like the sound of what his coach was saying. What was the point of wrestling if you didn't think you could win?

When the match began, Jeff's team had a two-point lead. At the heavier weight classes, Jeff's team had a good chance of winning big. As long as Jeff kept his match with Marcus close, his team would have a chance to win the meet itself.

When Jeff walked out on the mat, he felt like a scrawny kid next to Marcus. They were the same weight, but Marcus had broad shoulders and thick biceps. Jeff got even more nervous.

The Stallion wrestler flashed a confident grin. He shook hands with Jeff in the center of the ring.

Jeff waited for the whistle to blow. He did his best to block out everything, including his own nervousness.

Then the match started. He barely had any time to think.

Marcus was much stronger than Jeff was. Right away, Marcus charged at Jeff and tried to overpower him. He grabbed Jeff and picked him up off the ground. He threw him down hard, and Jeff felt the breath leave his lungs.

As he struggled to suck in air, Jeff also fought to keep from getting pinned. He pushed with his legs to try to keep Marcus away.

Jeff fought and pushed. As he tried to escape, he felt his face turning red.

I'm getting mad, he thought.

He focused on not losing his temper, not losing control. He tried to concentrate on escaping Marcus's grasp, pushing him away.

The flushed, angry feeling left Jeff's face. He carefully, quickly fought his way out from under Marcus's heavy arms.

Somehow, he made it through the first period. He got to the end without getting pinned. He'd lost the period, but not the match. He still had a shot.

As Jeff took a big sip of water between periods, he realized something important.

Wrestling Marcus was a lot like wrestling a stronger version of Brandon, the first person Jeff had wrestled. Marcus tried to use his strength to overpower Jeff, just like Brandon had.

But Brandon had not won because he was stronger. Brandon had only won because Jeff had gotten mad.

Suddenly, Jeff knew exactly what to do.

At the start of the second period, he held back, waiting for Marcus to charge. Sure enough, Marcus dove for Jeff's legs, just as Brandon had.

Jeff reacted quickly. He stepped out of the way. Then Jeff threw his weight on Marcus's back as he went by. He forced Marcus down on the mat.

Once Marcus was down, Jeff was in control. He wrapped up one of Marcus's legs and pushed his arm under him.

With one swift move — the same move Logan had used on the playground — Jeff flipped Marcus onto his back.

Now Marcus was struggling, and Jeff wasn't letting up. He forced Marcus down and held him steady. Marcus's shoulders dug into the mat.

The referee pounded the mat with his fist. "Pin!" he shouted.

Jeff leaped into the air. He'd won! Finally, he'd won a match. And he hadn't gotten angry at all!

Marcus rose and shook his hand. Then Jeff ran over to his teammates.

The other Pirate wrestlers surrounded him. The championship was theirs. Jeff had a huge smile on his face, and it matched the smiles on the faces of his teammates.

"Great job out there, Jeff," the coach said. "You made me proud. I think something clicked for you today!"

As the tired athletes walked out of the gym, Jeff heard someone say, "That new kid on the Pirates is great!"

Logan looked at Jeff and winked. "As long as you don't make him mad," Logan said.

ABOUT THE AUTHOR

Bob Temple lives in Rosemount, Minnesota, with his wife and three children. He has written more than thirty books for children. Over the years, he has coached more than twenty kids' soccer, basketball, and baseball teams. He also loves visiting classrooms to talk about his writing.

ABOUT THE ILLUSTRATOR

When Sean Tiffany was growing up, he lived on a small island off the coast of Maine. Every day, from sixth grade until he graduated from high school, he had to take a boat to get to school. When Sean isn't working on his art, he works on a multimedia project called "OilCan Drive," which combines music and art. He has a pet cactus named Jim.

.GLOSSARY.

experienced (ek-SPEER-ee-uhnssd)—if someone is experienced at something, they have a lot of knowledge and skill about it

focus (FOH-kuhss)—to concentrate

grasp (GRASP)—to grab and hold something

mat (MAT)—a large, thick floor pad used to protect wrestlers, gymnasts, and other athletes

opening stance (OH-puhn-ning STANSS)—in wrestling, the way that wrestlers stand at the beginning of a match

overpower (oh-vur-POW-ur)—to defeat someone by being stronger

period (PEER-ee-uhd)—one of the parts of a wrestling match

pin (PIN)—to win a wrestling match by holding your opponent to the ground

potential (puh-TEN-shuhl)—what you are capable of achieving in the future

takedown (TAYK-doun)—a move in which your opponent is quickly brought to the mat

temper (TEM-pur)—a tendency to get angry

HOW TO WIN

The basic goal of wrestling is to pin your opponent on his back so that both shoulders are touching the mat. If you do that, you win the match instantly. But wrestling matches are also timed, and you can win by scoring more points than your opponent during the match, too.

Matches are usually two or three rounds of two minutes each. You can get points by:

- **Takedowns** — bringing your opponent down to the mat

- **Reversals** — moving from defensive position to gaining control

- **Escapes** — getting away from your opponent's control

- **Exposure** — putting your opponent's back on the mat

ON THE WRESTLING MAT

There are some other ways to win a wrestling match.

- **Fall** — This is another word for "pin."

- **Technical Fall** — When one wrestler obtains a big lead in points, usually 10 or more, the match ends.

- **Decision** — The match ends because time runs out, and the winner is the one with the most points. In some cases, matches are decided by who wins the most rounds.

- **Major Decision** — The match ends because time runs out, and one wrestler holds a large lead in points, but not a big enough lead for a technical fall.

DISCUSSION QUESTIONS

1. Why is Jeff so angry with his little brother in the beginning of this book?

2. Why does Logan want to help Jeff?

3. Jeff goes through a big change in this book. What is it? Talk about the way that Jeff changes.

WRITING PROMPTS

1. What do you think will happen in Jeff's next wrestling match? Write a chapter that tells what happens.

2. Have you ever gotten mad at a younger sibling or a friend? Write about what happened. How did you resolve the problem?

3. Have you ever decided to try a new sport or activity? What activity or sport did you try? Write about your experience.

OTHER BOOKS

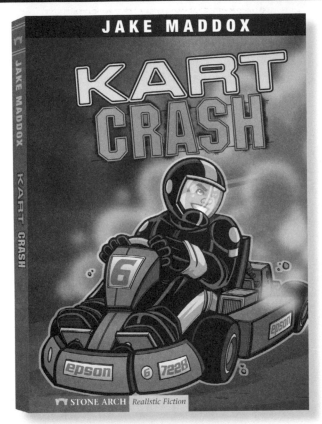

JAKE MADDOX

KART CRASH

JAKE MADDOX

KART CRASH

STONE ARCH *Realistic Fiction*

Austin had to leave his kart behind when he moved. He quickly learns that Ryan's the guy to beat at his new track. But how can Austin's rental kart compete with Ryan's fancy, shiny red kart? Is there any way Austin can win when he's facing the best?

BY JAKE MADDOX

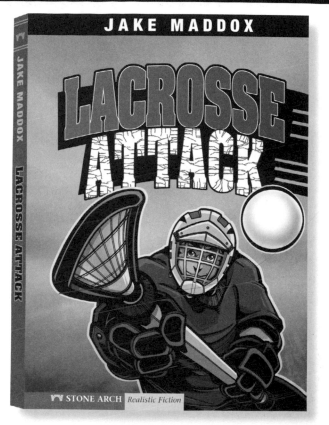

JAKE MADDOX

LACROSSE ATTACK

STONE ARCH *Realistic Fiction*

Peter made the varsity lacrosse team. But Hurley Johnson, the team's captain, doesn't want Peter to take his position. He'll stop at nothing to make Peter quit. Will Peter give up, or can he prove he deserves to be on the team?

INTERNET SITES

Do you want to know more about subjects related to this book? Or are you interested in learning about other topics? Then check out FactHound, a fun, easy way to find Internet sites.

Our investigative staff has already sniffed out great sites for you!

Here's how to use FactHound:

1. Visit *www.facthound.com*

2. Select your grade level.

3. To learn more about subjects related to this book, type in the book's ISBN number: **9781434207746**.

4. Click the **Fetch It** button.

FactHound will fetch the best Internet sites for you!